Follow Those Feet!

by Christine Ricci
illustrated by Susan Hall

SCHOLASTIC INC.

New York Toronto London Auckland Sydney
Mexico City New Delhi Hong Kong Buenos Aires

Based on the TV series *Dora the Explorer*® as seen on Nick Jr.®

ISBN 0-439-53979-X

12 11 10 9 8 7 6 5 4 3 2 1   3 4 5 6 7 8/0

Printed in the U.S.A.

First Scholastic printing, September 2003

Hi! I am .

DORA

 and I found

BOOTS

some in the .

FOOTPRINTS   SANDBOX

I wonder who made them.

Do you know?

Did I make these ?

FOOTPRINTS

No, my feet are small.
I did not make these .

FOOTPRINTS

Did  make these ?
BOOTS   **FOOTPRINTS**

No, his are shaped
FOOTPRINTS

like an oval. He did not

make these .
FOOTPRINTS

Who made these ? FOOTPRINTS

We can follow them to find out.

Hello, BIG RED CHICKEN !

Did you make these  ?

FOOTPRINTS

No, his feet have three
toes! He did not make
these .

FOOTPRINTS

Did the  make

HORSE

these ?

FOOTPRINTS

No, the horse wears  **HORSESHOES** on her feet. She did not make these . **FOOTPRINTS**

Did the  make these footprints?

No, the  CROCODILE has long nails. He did not make these FOOTPRINTS.

Did the 🐰 make the 👣 ?
RABBIT   FOOTPRINTS

No, she has two long feet

and two short feet.

She did not make these

FOOTPRINTS

Did the 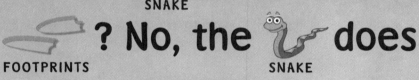 make these
SNAKE
 ? No, the  does

FOOTPRINTS   **SNAKE**

not have feet!

He slides across the ground. He did not make these .

FOOTPRINTS

Do you see ? Did
make these ?

SWIPER

SWIPER

FOOTPRINTS

No,  is sneaky!
SWIPER
He tiptoes. He did not
make these .
FOOTPRINTS

The  go all the way to
FOOTPRINTS
the beach!

They go by the 🐚🐚
SHELLS

toward the 🏰 .
SAND CASTLE

Now do you know who
made these ?
FOOTPRINTS

It was  ! He walked to
BENNY
the beach in his new  !
FLIPPERS

Yay! We did it! We found
out who made the  !

FOOTPRINTS